Dragonfly

and
the Web of Dreams

J. H. Sweet

Illustrated by Tara Larsen Chang

SOURCEBOOKS
Jabberwocky
AN IMPRINT OF SOURCEBOOKS

Published by Sourcebooks Jabberwocky, an imprint of Sourcebooks, Inc.
P.O. Box 4410, Naperville, Illinois 60567-4410
(630) 961-3900
Fax: (630) 961-2168
www.sourcebooks.com

Library of Congress Cataloging-in-Publication Data

Sweet, J. H.
  Dragonfly and the Web of Dreams / J.H. Sweet.
    p. cm.
  Summary: When the Web of Dreams is destroyed, Jennifer and her friends once again need to transform into fairies so they can contact the Dream Spider who is on holiday.
  ISBN-13: 978-1-4022-0873-7
  ISBN-10: 1-4022-0873-1
  [1. Fairies--Fiction. 2. Friendship--Fiction. 3. Dreams--Fiction.] I. Title.

PZ7.S9547Dr 2007
[Fic]--dc22

                                                    2006037110

Printed and bound in the United States of America.
LB 10 9 8 7 6 5 4 3 2 1

To Mom,
for good dreams

MEET THE

Marigold

NAME:
Beth Parish

FAIRY NAME AND SPIRIT:
Marigold

WAND:
Pussy Willow Branch

GIFT:
Can ward off nasty insects

MENTOR:
Aunt Evelyn,
Madam Monarch

Dragonfly

NAME:
Jennifer Sommerset

FAIRY NAME AND SPIRIT:
Dragonfly

WAND:
Peacock Feather

GIFT:
Very fast and very agile

MENTOR:
Grandmother,
Madam Chrysanthemum

FAIRY TEAM

Thistle

Firefly

NAME:
Grace Matthews

FAIRY NAME AND SPIRIT:
Thistle

WAND:
Porcupine Quill

GIFT:
Fierce and wild in
defending others

MENTOR:
Madam Robin

NAME:
Lenox Hart

FAIRY NAME AND SPIRIT:
Firefly

WAND:
Single Piece of Straw

GIFT:
A great light within

MENTOR:
Mrs. Pelter,
Madam June Beetle

Inside you is the power to do anything

The Fairy Chronicles

$\mathscr{C}$ontents

Chapter One

Saturday Morning

Early Saturday morning in September, Jennifer Sommerset sat on her porch, waiting for her three friends to arrive to spend the day. School had just started two weeks ago, and this was a special three-day weekend due to Labor Day. Jennifer had finished her homework the night before in anticipation of spending all of Saturday with her friends.

Her arm around one knee, the other leg dangling, she sat swinging in the porch swing and daydreaming about the summer fun she had had with her friends. Like many nine-year-olds, Jennifer spent the summer

swimming, skating, reading, climbing trees, playing video games, attending camp, and having sleepovers with friends. But she also did other activities that were very important, and some that were very secret.

Jennifer, along with her three friends, Grace Matthews, Lenox Hart, and Beth Parish, were all fairies. This meant that in addition to being normal girls, they were also blessed with fairy spirits.

Jennifer's fairy spirit was that of a red dragonfly. In fairy form, her wings and dress were a dark, blood red color. Her dress came to just above her knees and was made of soft velvety fuzz. Jennifer was a tall, athletic black girl with short dark hair combed into tiny waves very close to her head. She liked to keep her hair short because she was always busy with a lot of activities. It was easier to play soccer and swim with short hair. And it was convenient not to have her hair in her face while flying around on fairy business. Jennifer was very striking and beautiful, both as a regular girl and as a fairy. She carried herself with poise and confidence, and was a natural leader.

Grace was a thistle fairy, lived four blocks away, and was Jennifer's best friend. They both went to Memorial Elementary School and had known each other for three years.

Lenox was a firefly fairy. She was home-schooled by her mother. But Lenox's mother kept the same schedule as the public schools, so Lenox got to spend time with her friends on weekends, holidays, and in the summer.

Beth was a marigold fairy and lived farther across town. She attended Belaire Elementary. Jennifer had met Lenox and Beth at Fairy Circles, which were gatherings of fairies. Beth had been the most recent fairy to join their group this past summer. Dragonfly, Thistle, Firefly, and

Marigold had all participated in a daring mission to help the brownies (boy fairies) rescue the Feather of Hope from a house occupied by dangerous gremlins. Then Jennifer and Beth went to Camp Hopi at the same time and signed up to be tent-mates. They had a lot of fun hiking, swimming, biking, and learning how to make candles and baskets.

Jennifer was very excited that her friends were coming to spend the day. They would probably play games and get out beads to make jewelry in the morning. After lunch, Jennifer's grandmother was going to teach the young fairies some new wand tricks.

Jennifer's grandmother was a yellow chrysanthemum fairy and was Jennifer's mentor. She was Madam Mum to the other fairies, but Jennifer called her Grandmum.

All young fairies were assigned a mentor as a teacher and supervisor.

Wand magic could be complicated and dangerous. So far, the younger fairies had only learned simple wand tricks like how to produce fairy lights and how to fix broken items.

Fairies were problem solvers and spent a lot of time fixing things. It was also their job to protect nature. But fairies were never allowed to use their magic for trivial things, or to abuse others. In fact, young fairies could not use magic at all without permission from their mentors. So the girls were all very much looking forward to learning something new from an older fairy.

Fairy wands could be made from almost any object and were bewitched to help fairies perform magic. Jennifer's wand was an enchanted peacock feather. It was very beautiful and full of peacock enchantment. If it got upset, it could scream loudly, just like the cry of a peacock. But most of the time it was very serious, and proud to be helping Dragonfly carry out important fairy business. Jennifer usually kept her wand in the belt of her fairy dress along with a pouch of pixie dust and her fairy handbook.

Pixie dust was needed to help fairies perform fairy magic, and the handbook contained information and answers to fairy questions. The fairy handbook was a unique book because it had the ability to age with its owner. Right now, Jennifer's handbook contained definitions and descriptions that a nine-year-old could understand. As Jennifer got older, and needed help making more mature decisions, the information in the handbook would change and become more detailed.

None of the girls' parents knew about fairy things. In fact, to regular people, fairies looked just like flowers, insects, tree blossoms, reptiles, berries, and small animals. Jennifer's mother had seen her daughter in fairy form before, but had only recognized her as a red dragonfly.

Jennifer's daydreaming was interrupted when her mother came out of the house in her bathrobe to pick up the newspaper from the front steps. Mrs. Sommerset was a dentist and was getting ready to go to work. She kept her office open every other Saturday. Jennifer's father was a lawyer and had already left for his office. He was busy preparing a big case for trial and had to work over the holiday weekend. While her parents worked, Jennifer's grandmother looked after her. She was a widow and had lived with the family since before Jennifer was born.

Mrs. Sommerset was looking out over the large garden plot on the left side of the house. "I thought I asked you to pick up all of those boots last week," she said to Jennifer.

"You missed one." With that, Mrs. Sommerset went back inside to finish dressing.

For nearly two years, Mrs. Sommerset had been putting old boots in her garden. She had read somewhere that this would help scare rabbits away, and keep them from eating her vegetables and flowers. Well, she had tried it. But it didn't work. She finally gave up last week and told Jennifer to pick up all the boots and put them in the garden shed.

Looking out over the garden, Jennifer couldn't see the boot her mother was referring to. All she could see was Mr. Wimple, the garden gnome, who came every Saturday on his garden route to help tend to the Sommersets' garden. He helped the plants grow and added colors to nature. This was the job of gnomes. Last week, Mr. Wimple had changed the bark of the peach tree to the exact color of milk chocolate, and had made the fuzz on the

MR WIMPLE
the Garden Gnome

okra a misty green color. Currently, he was doing something with the row of asparagus.

Jennifer smiled. To regular humans, a gnome would appear as an ordinary object like a rock, a pumpkin, or a soccer ball. Mr. Wimple had taken to disguising himself as a boot in Mrs. Sommerset's garden.

Garden gnomes pretty much all looked similar. About ten inches high, they were a dusty brown color all over, including their boots and clothes. Garden gnomes didn't have beards like wood and mountain gnomes. But they did have very thick, bushy moustaches.

Mr. Wimple was dressed in traditional gnome work clothes: overalls with lots of pockets and rolled up pant cuffs. In his pockets and pant cuffs, he stored various tools, gloves, bulbs, seeds, and other things needed for his job.

Jennifer left the porch and went to talk to Mr. Wimple. "Hi, Mr. Wimple," she said.

Then, laughing a little, she added, "I'm sorry to have to tell you this, but Mom wants you out of the garden."

Mr. Wimple stopped digging for a moment to study Jennifer. Then he said, "Well I can't leave just now. I'm thinning these asparagus crowns. They are too crowded. She could lose the whole row if I don't get it done."

As he paused in his work, the gnome took a handkerchief out of one of his pockets and wiped his face. After looking around the garden for a few moments, Mr. Wimple smiled and added, "So she's not putting out boots anymore. I could have told her it wouldn't work. Rabbits are too smart, and boots are too dumb. The only thing that works is to plant a little extra for the rabbits."

Jennifer laughed at this and asked, "Do you think you could look like something else for awhile, maybe a cabbage, so Mom will think I put all the boots away like she asked?"

Mr. Wimple smiled again and answered, "One cabbage coming up." He closed his eyes and screwed up his face tight. After a few seconds, he opened his eyes and took a deep breath. "There," he said.

Jennifer couldn't tell any difference, except that he had taken on a slight, pale green tinge. "Thank you," said Jennifer.

Before she could turn to go back to the porch, Mr. Wimple told her, "Now golf shoes are smarter than boots. You know, because of the spikes. They are good for the yard. Some of the smartest people wear golf shoes when mowing their lawns. It helps to aerate, to get oxygen down into the soil. Grass roots need oxygen."

Mr. Wimple liked to talk and could be a

little long-winded. Jennifer listened politely as he went on. "I've got to get this done pretty quickly today. I'm trying to get a few gardens ahead in my work. I'm taking tomorrow off to go to the annual Garden Gnome Convention out on Mr. Henderson's farm. There should be some really exciting new things this year."

He paused and sighed before going on. "But I'm feeling a little tired today. I had a bad dream last night and couldn't sleep: monster fungus and giant tomato worms destroying all of the gardens on my route." He shivered a little, shaking his head, and began digging again.

Jennifer frowned as she wandered back to the porch. It was probably just a coincidence that she also had a bad dream last night, but something was troubling her.

Chapter Two

Fairy Friends

itting in the swing, deep in thought, Jennifer didn't notice Grace had arrived until she was already on the porch. Since they only lived a few blocks apart, the girls usually walked or rode bicycles to visit each other. Grace had walked this morning. She was carrying a bag and said, "I brought some beads, so we don't use up all of yours."

Jennifer looked through the bead bag while Grace went to say hi to Mr. Wimple. "Hi, Mr. Wimple."

"Hello, Thistle," he answered.

Mr. Wimple also visited the Matthews' house on his route, usually on Tuesdays.

Gnome Convention

A gathering of gnomes that usually occurs once a year. There are four separate gnome conventions, one for each of the Gnome divisions: Garden, Wood, Mountain & Desert...

Grace's mom and dad only planted bushes and flowers, so it was a much smaller job than the Sommersets' garden. Mr. Wimple usually made it a point to look like a croquet mallet while in the Matthews' yard since Grace had a croquet set.

Mr. Wimple went on to tell Grace how excited he was to be attending the annual Garden Gnome Convention on Sunday, and further explained his hopes for all kinds of new tools and techniques.

When Mr. Wimple went back to digging up asparagus crowns, Grace returned to the porch. "I was just hearing about the gnome convention," she told Jennifer.

Jennifer took out her fairy handbook, looked up gnome convention, and read the handbook's entry aloud to Grace:

"*Gnome Convention: A gathering of gnomes that usually occurs once a year. There are four separate gnome* conventions, one for each of the gnome divisions: garden, wood, mountain, and desert. The Garden Gnome Convention this year is scheduled for Sunday, September 4, and will be held on Mr. Henderson's farm. The gnomes will visit with each other, and exchange ideas on growing techniques and new ways of adding colors to nature. In addition, they will attend workshops led by gnome inventors with specific areas of expertise, who have developed new and improved tools and methods to carry out gnome job functions. This year's highly anticipated classes include Fertilizer Developments, Advanced Gardening Technology, and Concentrated Gnome Magic. There will also be a special seed, root, nut, and bulb trading session."

"Wow!" exclaimed Grace. "No wonder Mr. Wimple is so excited." Then she pulled out her porcupine quill wand and began polishing it on the hem of her t-shirt.

Grace loved her wand and tried to take good care of it. Her wand wasn't the only thing about her that was sharp and pointy. In fact, in fairy form, Thistle was prickly all over. She had short, spiky blond hair and tall, pointed, feathery gray wings. And her dress was made of sharp, pale purple thistle petals.

Grace had large gray eyes, full of laughter and expression. Of all the fairies, she was the one who got along best with the brownies. She thought that their mischief and pranks were very funny. But she was also very capable of playing tricks herself, and her special fairy gift was the ability to fiercely defend against attack if needed. So nothing much bothered her.

Jennifer's special fairy gift was speed and agility, just like the abilities of a dragonfly.

She was so fast and coordinated that no one could ever catch her. This was a great asset to her soccer game. In fact, she was so good that her PE teacher had already encouraged her to think about the possibility of future soccer scholarships.

Both Jennifer and Grace got very excited when a lime green station wagon pulled into the driveway. Beth's Aunt Evelyn was driving. She was a monarch butterfly fairy and was Beth's mentor. The younger fairies respectfully called her Madam Monarch, except for Beth, who still called her Aunt Evelyn. Beth and her aunt had picked up Lenox on the way. Now that everyone had arrived, they could start having fun.

"Hello, Jennifer," said Aunt Evelyn. "I need to speak to your grandmother. Is she home?"

Opening the front door, Jennifer pointed. "She's all the way back, on the left." Jennifer's grandmother had her own apartment with a kitchen and bath built onto the back of the house.

Jennifer's mother had stepped onto the porch just as her daughter opened the door, and after a quick greeting to all of the guests, she left for work.

After she had driven away, there were four small *pops* as the girls all transformed into fairies. Standard fairy form was six inches. They sat on the porch railing together, watching Mr. Wimple finish his work.

Lenox was a golden brown firefly fairy. She glowed from head to toe and had shoulder length, straight auburn hair. Her wings were sparkling gold; and her dress was a satiny, golden brown silk, spun especially for her by a friendly silkworm. For her wand, she carried a single piece of bright gleaming straw.

Lenox's fairy gift was a light greater than any other fairy. It lit dark places, helped to guide her, and seldom allowed her to be misled by bad spirits.

As a marigold fairy, Beth had a crown of
tiny yellow flowers and wore a dress made of
crinkly, yellow and gold marigold petals. She
had short, curly, light brown hair and pale gold

wings. Her wand was an enchanted pussy
willow branch. It liked to purr when petted.

Beth's fairy gift was the ability to ward off
unfriendly insects like wasps, locusts, and fire

ants. Marigold flowers had this quality in nature. Many people planted them in their gardens to keep bugs from eating the flowers and vegetables. Unlike most people, Beth never got bit by chiggers or mosquitoes.

Mr. Wimple had finished his work and stopped to say goodbye. His pockets and pant cuffs were stuffed full of the thinned asparagus crowns. He told the girls, "I'm taking these extra crowns over to Mrs. Harrison's garden. She doesn't plant asparagus, but she loves volunteers." Mr. Wimple went on to explain, "Volunteers are plants and vegetables that grow without being planted. They are usually seeds blown in from other gardens or carried in by birds and squirrels that sprout on their own.

"This will be quite a treat for Mrs. Harrison. She'll be so happy, she might even cry. She thinks volunteer vegetables are magical."

With a last wave goodbye to the fairies, Mr. Wimple set off at a trot toward his next garden.

Chapter Three

Bad Dreams

After Mr. Wimple left, Thistle said to Dragonfly, "You look tired, Jennifer."

Jennifer responded, "Well, I always have trouble getting to sleep. My mind is too active. My parents call me a thinker. I'm always thinking up ideas and making plans in my head." She paused before she went on. "But the last two nights I've had nightmares, and I couldn't get back to sleep. I guess that's why I'm a little tired. It's the same falling-elevator dream I've had since I was five. I already know it's going to fall, but I get in anyway."

"I've been having bad dreams too," said Firefly. "Mine are about mummies. Mom tells me I watch too many movies, but it's funny that we are both having bad dreams."

"Well, you may not believe this," Thistle said, "but I had a nightmare last night too." Her gray eyes were even larger than normal as she explained further. "I've had the same dream off and on for over a week. The porcupine is coming for his missing quill. He attacks. But I only have one quill, and he has thousands. It's pretty scary."

Dragonfly looked up nightmares in her fairy handbook and read the entry to her friends:

"*Nightmares: Nightmares are bad dreams caused by Drommelak, an evil dream spirit that descends on sleeping creatures. Most nightmares are caught by the Web of Dreams, which is a magical web cast by the Dream Spider. Good dreams ride on the wings of doves.*"

The fairies sat thinking about this for a few moments. Eventually, all eyes turned to Beth, who had not yet said anything about her dreams.

When she still didn't say anything, Firefly finally asked, "Are you having bad dreams too, Marigold?"

When Beth still didn't answer, the other girls continued to stare expectantly at her. Finally, she couldn't stand it anymore and blurted out, "Okay, I admit I'm having bad dreams. But it's not something I want to share with everyone." She walked a little ways down the porch railing and stared off into the yard.

The other fairies looked at each other, surprised and concerned.

"It must be pretty bad," Thistle said quietly.

To draw the subject away from bad dreams, and Beth, Lenox said, "Jennifer, your house is amazing. It's so huge."

The house *was* a very large three-story house with big rooms, high ceilings, wide halls, and a wrap-around porch. It also had a separate garage, workshop, and garden shed. Jennifer shrugged and responded, "Bigger isn't always better. I've gotten lost in there before. That's not good, is it?" After thinking for a while, she added, "But I did learn to skate in the hallways. That was pretty neat. And there is plenty of room for my recycle bins. Let me give you a little tour of the recycle storage area."

The fairies transformed back to normal girl size and followed Jennifer into the house. She led them to the combination pantry and laundry room. It was very large, and one whole wall was devoted to color-coded recycle bins.

Jennifer was very environmentally conscious, most fairies were. But Jennifer took her duties to the extreme. She had

bins for newspaper, plastic containers, steel cans, magazines, plastic bags, writing paper, cardboard, aluminum cans, and glass. Jennifer also reused things whenever she could. Her room was filled with jars and plastic butter tubs that held things like beads, shells, string, and crayons.

Jennifer had also authored a pamphlet called *51 Ways to Reuse Coffee Cans*. She had distributed it at school and to her friends at Fairy Circle. Because of this, Lenox's mom now used a coffee can for a step stool in the bathroom, to reach the towels in the top cabinet. It was just the right size to be stored under the sink when not in use. And Beth's mother now stored dog food in coffee cans for their dachshund, Peanut. This kept ants from getting into the food, and the cans were easy to pour from. Jennifer was working on a new brochure due out around December—*102 Uses for Butter Tubs*.

Pulling an item out of her pocket, Jennifer said, "I can't figure out what to do with this." It was a rubber ring from a canning jar that was split, and could no longer be used as a canning seal for preserves, pickles, and jams. "We can't recycle rubber yet. But this is just like a strong rubber band. I should be able to use it for something." She shoved it back into her pocket with a shrug of her shoulders.

As a final bit of recycling information, Jennifer told her friends, "I've been forbidden to harass Mr. Longfellow across the street." When her friends looked at her questioningly, Jennifer explained, "He was throwing out all kinds of plastic. So a couple of months ago I gave him a lecture on how bad plastic is in a landfill. Glass and paper are not as bad for landfills, but plastic is horrible. He doesn't seem to be throwing away as much plastic as before. So maybe I did some good.

"But I'm not allowed to bother him, so I've had to get sneaky. He's still throwing away newspapers, so yesterday I asked him if I could collect his used newspapers once a week for a school project. I'll just add them to ours and recycle them." Jennifer finished, looking very pleased with herself.

The other fairies did admire Jennifer's dedication and hard work, but they doubted if they would be brave enough to lecture grown-up neighbors, and they were a little surprised that she was looking through other people's garbage.

Just as the girls were getting ready to spread out beads and other jewelry-making supplies on the kitchen table, Madam Monarch and Madam Mum came down the hallway.

"Girls, we are going to an emergency Fairy Circle," said Madam Mum, adding, "There is an urgent problem we need to discuss."

"Does it have anything to do with nightmares?" Jennifer asked, looking sideways at Beth.

There was quiet for a few moments, and then glancing at Madam Mum, Madam Monarch responded, "As usual, they are one step ahead of us. Yes, it's about the nightmares. Quickly now, we need to leave. We are going on a difficult and important mission that will take two days."

As the girls were gathering up their bead boxes and bags, Madam Monarch told Grace, Beth, and Lenox, "I have already contacted your parents. I asked them if you could do a two-night sleepover at my house, and told them that we would all be going swimming and to a craft fair. I will be calling them periodically to check in, so they won't worry if they call my house and we're not there."

Beth's aunt lived alone, so she could embark on fairy adventures without being missed by anyone. This also made her house the perfect cover for the other fairies.

As they were heading out the front door, Madam Mum told Jennifer, "I called your mom at work, so she knows."

They locked up the house and left quickly, piling into the lime green station wagon and buckling up.

Beth sat in the back seat and scrunched herself into the corner against the door. She sighed and thought about her night-mares. For the last three nights, she dreamed that she was with her friends on a fairy adventure. But Dragonfly was caught in a spider web with an enormous spider advancing towards her. Marigold was supposed to be able to ward off spiders with her fairy gift. But she was frozen with fear, unable to move, unable to help. Firefly couldn't do anything against the spider. She didn't have the power. Thistle was battling the spider alone, but she was too small and needed help. Even with her fierceness, Thistle couldn't save Dragonfly by herself. She needed Marigold to help.

Beth had only learned that she was a fairy this summer. Since then, she had never had a test of her fairy power. Could it be that she would fail in the face of danger? Would her friends perish because she lacked courage?

Beth was so upset and worried that she got flushed, couldn't breathe, and shook all over. She was terrified. Several hot tears rolled down her cheeks. She kept her face to the car window.

Jennifer, who was sitting next to Beth, noticed something was wrong, but didn't say anything. Instead, she put her arm around Beth's shoulders and gave her a small hug.

Chapter Four

Fairy Circle

Only about fifteen fairies were able to attend Fairy Circle on such short notice. The fairies had met under a willow tree at their last Fairy Circle, to brainstorm and problem solve because willow trees inspire communication and creative ideas. They met under an oak tree this time in a small area of woods outside of town.

Oak trees were full of wisdom and visions of the future, and the fairies hoped this would help with making decisions and plans. But oak trees usually only gave advice in the form of complicated riddles that were not often solved quickly enough to be helpful to anyone.

Since oak trees could see the future, they were afraid of giving out too much information. They learned long ago that with the ability to predict the future, they were in danger of changing it by giving advice that might influence actions. In giving complex riddles instead, many people would give up trying to solve them, and would eventually forget them. And others would take so long to work them out that the future events would have already happened by the time the riddles were solved. Still, it was encouraging for the fairies to

be sitting under such immense wisdom and knowledge.

Dragonfly recognized many of the other fairies at Fairy Circle including Lily, Primrose, Spiderwort, Periwinkle, Tulip, Morning Glory, and Madam June Beetle, who was Firefly's neighbor and mentor.

Thistle's mentor had also arrived. Not all fairy mentors were fairies. Thistle's mentor was a robin. Madam Robin was very old and wise; and she could talk, which was very rare. Animals and birds could only speak if they were bewitched. This meant that Madam Robin had been put under a spell at some time. No one seemed to know the bewitching story, so Madam Robin was very mysterious and exciting to the young fairies.

Madam Toad was the leader of the fairies in this region. As a magnificent, muddy colored, greenish-brown toad fairy, she was very impressive. She wore a pale green dress, sparkling with moisture drops and had small, dark green wings perched on her plump shoulders. Madam Toad carried a miniature red rosebud-stem wand and had a crown of tiny rosebuds to match. Her gigantic black eyes glittered brightly, and her voice was very strong and commanding. She began the meeting with a loud croak and called out, "Welcome, welcome! Attention, attention everyone! We are here to discuss the problem of the nightmares. First of all, we need to thank the doves."

Madam Toad gestured to one side of the gathering where several tired and bedraggled looking doves were cooing sleepily. "They have been working overtime, delivering good dreams to help balance out the dream problem. It would be much worse if not for their efforts."

There was polite applause and Madam Toad continued. "The Web of Dreams has been destroyed. I went with the Sandman

yesterday to confirm this. It is not clear who destroyed it, or how anyone knew its location. But it must be rebuilt quickly or the problem will worsen. I have been in contact with Mother Nature."

The fairies all looked at each other. It was very rare for any creature to meet with Mother Nature. She was the guardian of many magical spirits and beings like fairies, brownies, elves, gnomes, leprechauns, dwarves, and trolls; and she was the supervisor of all nature activities. But she was very dangerous; and it was not possible to predict when she would be in a safe form like dew, breeze, or drizzle. Mother Nature was often in dangerous forms like hail, geyser, and avalanche.

Madam Toad went on. "Fortunately, she was in rainbow form when I talked to her. She gave me the schedule and location of the Dream Spider. He is in the far North and is currently on holiday. We must set out to see him at once. The journey is a long one and will require an overnight stay in the forest near the Dream Spider's home. The fairy group will leave immediately after the meeting, travel the rest of today, and meet with the spider in the morning.

"It is too far for fairies to fly alone, and speed is very important in this matter. The brownies have agreed to help us. They have arranged our transportation for the journey."

For the first time, the fairies noticed two brownies in the shadows behind Madam Toad. Behind the brownies stood a falcon and a barn owl. Since brownies didn't have wings and couldn't fly, they rode on birds and animals to travel. Dragonfly recognized one of the brownies from their summer Fairy Circle.

Madam Toad introduced the Fairy Circle visitors. "You remember Brownie Christopher, and this is Brownie Stephen."

Brownies derived their spirits from

things like pinecones, mushrooms, and other natural, earthy things. They were seven inches high and almost always wore tan and brown colored clothes.

Christopher and Stephen were both dressed in tan. Christopher was a brown-haired acorn brownie and wore an acorn cap for a hat. Stephen was a red-haired river stone brownie. He wore a string of polished river stones around his neck. They both shuffled their feet and stuffed their hands into their pockets, blushing and looking down as they were introduced.

Madam Toad further explained, "Christopher and Stephen have very kindly discussed the situation with their bird friends. The owl and falcon have agreed to carry the fairies safely to and from the Dream Spider's home. I have given the birds the location and directions.

"I have decided that the group to make the journey will consist of Dragonfly, Thistle, Marigold, and Firefly, because of their special fairy gifts. The Dream Spider is not the friendliest fellow and will not take kindly to being disturbed. Dragonfly will be able to talk to him, and with her speed, also stay out of his reach. Thistle and Marigold will ward him off if needed. And Firefly's light will prove invaluable for the entire journey. Madam Mum, Madam Monarch, and Madam Robin will supervise.

"For those of you who have never met the Sandman, let me introduce him."

the Sandman

With this, the Sandman stepped out from behind the trunk of the oak tree. He was a little taller than a foot, probably fourteen inches or so, and was a glittery sand color all over. The Sandman was very thin, and if he had been standing completely still, the fairies would have thought he was a tall, man-shaped sandcastle. His hat and shoes were pointy; and he had a long beard, curled in a spiral like a corkscrew that reached all the way to his pointed toes. He nodded hello to all of them and politely waited for Madam Toad to continue speaking.

"The Sandman will accompany the group on the trip, since he is directly concerned with sleep and dreams."

Dragonfly hurriedly looked up Sandman in her fairy handbook:

Sandman: A magical being whose job is to help induce sleep. He travels the world, putting creatures of

all kinds to sleep by tossing magical
sleep sand into their eyes.

Dragonfly was thinking what an amazing creature the Sandman was. Since she often had difficulty getting to sleep, she thought it would be wonderful to have a visit from the Sandman once in awhile. But she wondered if sleep sand would actually work for her, since it was usually her active mind that kept her awake.

Madam Toad was just about to go on, when a curious phenomenon swept through the Fairy Circle. All of the fairies began itching, and with the itching began the scratching. Within just a few seconds, there was so much itching and scratching that no one could think properly.

Brownie Stephen was giggling madly. Several moments before, he had sped around the outer edge of the Fairy Circle and tossed a bit of itching powder onto each fairy.

Brownie Christopher chided him. "This was no time for a prank, Stephen!" But Christopher was smiling. Then he started sniggering.

Rather than risk getting into more trouble, or having to face the full power of the fairies' wrath, the brownies decided to leave. A fox suddenly appeared from the shadowy woods, and the brownies swung themselves onto his back.

Christopher called to Madam Toad. "We must go now. No need for thanks. The owl and falcon know what to do." With that, the fox left quickly with a flick of his fluffy red tail.

The itchy fairies were very agitated. But Madam Toad took control. Her voice was very loud and commanding. "Calm down! I will take care of this." She waved her rose-bud wand in tiny figure-eights, uttering, *"Permanent scratch, permanent scratch."*

Little gray wisps, like smoke rings in figure-eight shapes, appeared and traveled out from her wand to the rest of the fairies. As soon as the wisps reached the fairies, their itching stopped.

Most of the fairies were very angry, but not Thistle. She loved brownie mischief. In fact, she was laughing so hard that she was rolling on the ground, holding her stomach.

Madam Toad addressed the fairies. "Before this summer, brownies were never invited to Fairy Circle. When they asked for our help with the Feather of Hope, they restrained themselves from pulling any pranks. Now we have asked for their help, and they provided it. This was easily fixable. And remember, brownies cannot help themselves when it comes to pranks. I'm afraid in the interest of teamwork, we must put up with a little brownie mischief."

Thistle had finally gotten herself under control. She stood up, her eyes still watering with laughter, and brushed her dress off. Her friends had to smile.

Backpacks had already been packed for the fairies. Each contained a pillow, a blanket, water, peanut butter and marshmallow créme sandwiches, lemon jellybeans, powdered sugar puff pastries, and raspberries. And Madam Mum had a large thermos of coffee. "I can't make it without my caffeine," she said.

After Dragonfly put on her backpack, she slung the fire shield she had brought to Fairy Circle across her back. The fire shield was about the size of a large coin and was used to protect the earth from scarring when building a fairy campfire. Dragonfly had decided to bring her fire shield to every Fairy Circle in case they needed to build a fire. It was made of iron and had a chain attached for easy carrying. With the fire shield slung across her back, Dragonfly looked like a little warrior, ready for battle.

When they were ready to go, it was decided that the barn owl would carry the

Sandman, Thistle would ride on Madam Robin, and the rest of the fairies would travel on the falcon. Since the fairies were small and light, the falcon was easily able to carry five at once.

Madam Toad addressed Madam Monarch. "If you'll give me your keys, Evelyn, I will make sure your car gets home, so you can go straight there when you return."

Then the fairy leader bid them farewell. "Flitter forth fairies and take care of business. And good luck. The doves will continue to work hard until the web is rebuilt. But be quick and convincing. The Dream Spider must come at once."

The rest of the fairies waved and wished them luck too as the group took flight.

Chapter Five

The Journey

No one of the fairies had ever flown this high before. And Thistle was the only one who had ever traveled on the back of a bird. It was wonderful. Even though the rushing air was cool, the feathers of the falcon kept them warm.

Madam Robin flew next to the falcon. They led the way, and the barn owl brought up the rear. The Sandman didn't care much for flying and had his arms wrapped tightly around the neck of the owl. Dragonfly had flown in a plane before, but this was a much better view.

They were higher than fairies normally flew, but lower than planes. The landscape looked like a giant patchwork quilt, and the colors were beautiful. They saw an aqua lake, an emerald forest, a silver river, and a golden hay field. Over valleys, hills, streams, highways, woods, and houses, they soared. At one point, the fairies passed several very tired-looking doves flying in the opposite direction. Madam Robin sang an encouraging note to them, and they cooed back to her.

For a while, no one said anything. They just admired the view in silent appreciation. But Dragonfly had been waiting for an opportunity to tease Marigold about her friendship with Brownie Alan.

Alan was the new keeper of the Feather of Hope. The fairies had met him over the summer, and he really liked Marigold. Dragonfly knew that Alan and Marigold had been sending nut messages back and forth to each other for the last two months.

Nut messages were hollowed-out nuts used for fairy communication. Letters and notes were secreted inside the nuts, and birds and animals delivered them for the fairies.

Hiding her smile, and keeping her voice very serious, Dragonfly asked Marigold, "Have you heard from Alan lately? What's he up to?"

Marigold answered, "Oh yes. I had two messages from him last week. He's still spreading hope with the feather. He'll be on feather duty until December.

"He's had quite a few adventures lately. An egret dropped him in a muddy cattle field. Evidently, egrets like to hang out with cattle, but they don't much like to carry brownies. And an osprey dropped him in a lake. The osprey forgot he was carrying him and dove for a fish. But he's had some good experiences too. A really nice beaver helped him cross a river. And he is now on his way to Patagonia by means of dolphins and

whales. They only have to go there once a year. Apparently, the higher they fly with the feather, the more hope is spread and the longer it lasts. He can get pretty high over the Andes on a giant condor."

Marigold paused, breathless. Then she noticed the other girls were giggling, and she heard a little chorus of, *"Beth has a boyfriend. Beth has a boyfriend."*

Marigold blushed a little. Looking away and rolling her eyes, she tried to ignore them.

Madam Mum said, "Girls, stop teasing." But she and Madam Monarch were both smiling.

After a while, the fairies started to get bored. Dragonfly had brought some string with her, so they all played cat's cradle and other string games for about an hour.

Dragonfly was sitting next to Firefly and noticed that her friend was more quiet than usual. "What's the matter, Lenox?" she asked.

Firefly answered quietly, "I don't know. Something's wrong. I mean, even more wrong than all of the nightmares and the destruction of the Web of Dreams." She thought for a few moments before saying, "My light is telling me that we are being misled. But I don't understand it. Misled by whom? Everyone here is trustworthy, right?"

"I think so," Dragonfly answered. After thinking a while, she asked, "Have you ever been this far North before? Maybe it's a distance or direction thing."

"You're probably right," Firefly said, sighing. "I just don't like this feeling."

The girls stopped talking when they noticed the Sandman looking at them.

As dusk approached, Firefly began to glow more brightly to provide light; and the fairies took out their wands. Madam Mum had a pine needle wand, and Madam Monarch carried a single dandelion seed. When each of the fairies whispered the words, "*Fairy light*," the tips of their wands glowed softly.

The owl, the falcon, and Madam Robin did not need light to fly. But being far from home, and high in the air, the fairies felt better with a bit of extra light for comfort.

Chapter Six

Trolls

 bout an hour after dark, the birds descended and landed in the woods.

Madam Mum told the others, "We will make camp here tonight. In the morning, the falcon and owl will show us where the Dream Spider resides."

The owl and falcon left to find food and water, and the Sandman went off for a little walk to stretch his legs while the fairies unpacked their backpacks.

On the mossy side of a tree trunk, they each chose a soft little niche between the tree roots, and put out their blankets and pillows. Then they unpacked their provisions. The fairies were especially looking forward to the lemon jellybeans because all fairies loved lemon jellybeans. They ate their peanut butter and marshmallow créme sandwiches first, saving the jellybeans for last.

Dragonfly gathered dried twigs, leaves, and small branches, and placed them in the shallow bowl of the fire shield. Madam Mum stood close by to supervise while

Dragonfly waved her peacock feather wand over the kindling and uttered, "*Ignite.*"

A small fire sprang up to light the camp and warm the chilly fairies.

Madam Mum told Dragonfly, "Good job, dear." After watching the flames for a few moments, she added, "Just a reminder. The only time you can perform that wand trick is with an older fairy present."

Dragonfly smiled and answered, "I remember, Grandmum."

Madam Monarch and Madam Robin returned from a scouting trip around the perimeter of the camp. Madam Robin told the fairies, "We've spotted several piles of leaves and acorns, and a stack of branches. This may mean that trolls are close by. Trolls are not usually dangerous, but they are curious. We will need to keep fairly quiet."

Dragonfly sat down cross-legged and looked up trolls in her fairy handbook. She noticed that Thistle and Marigold were also thumbing through their handbooks, and Firefly was looking over Thistle's shoulder. Since she didn't need to read aloud to her friends, Dragonfly read the entry to herself:

> *Trolls:* *Trolls are magical creatures about four feet high, and almost as wide. They have eight fingers and eight toes, and live mainly in dens and caves in the woods. They sleep during the day. If they get caught in the sunlight, they will turn to stone. Trolls like to pile and stack things such as leaves, stones, and branches. They are easily confused and have poor memories, often requiring constant reminders.*

Dragonfly had a very active imagination. As she sat thinking about trolls, she thought she was daydreaming when three large trolls ran into their camp. She only realized they were real when the others gave frightened squeals.

Each troll carried a glass bell jar. And before the fairies and Madam Robin could fly out of reach, they were all covered with the jars. Madam Robin and Thistle were under one jar. Madam Monarch, Firefly, and Madam Mum were under the second jar. And Marigold and Dragonfly were trapped under the third one.

"We got them!" cried one of the trolls. She was a young girl troll, and the other two looked about the right ages to be her parents.

They all had bushy blond hair and eyebrows, and large noses. The trolls were dressed in soft, comfortable looking clothes that included pants, pullovers, vests, and shoes, in mixed-up woodsy colors like mustard, cranberry, olive, chocolate, cinnamon, pumpkin, and celery.

Next, the three trolls sat down in front of the jars and stared at the fairies.

Finally, the father troll spoke. "Every time there is a problem, fairies are always around." He shook his head and paused before addressing the fairies again. Then he gestured to the girl troll and said, "My Esmerelda has been having the worst day-mares. She's never had bad dreams before. And here you are. Fairies! You must be causing this problem."

Before he could go on, and before any of the bell-jarred fairies could speak, two more fairies flew into their camp. One was a tiny shrew fairy. She was a glistening, silvery brown color and carried a red tulip wand. The other was a milkweed fairy with black hair. She carried a pheasant feather wand; and her dress was made of long, silky-white milkweed strands.

Hovering in front of the man troll's face, Madam Shrew pointed her wand at

him and commanded loudly, "Release them! Release them at once, and we will talk." When he hesitated, she shouted, "*NOW!*"

Apparently, the trolls had a healthy respect for the shrew fairy because they all three jumped up and quickly lifted the jars, setting them aside. Then they sat back down, looking sheepish while Madam Shrew introduced herself to the other fairies. "I am Madam Shrew, and this is Milkweed. I'm the leader of fairies for this region. I just received a nut message from Madam Toad. We have come to help you."

Madam Shrew and Milkweed shook hands with the other fairies. Milkweed was a little older than Dragonfly, Thistle, Marigold, and Firefly. As she shook hands with them, she said, "I'm Caitlin. Madam Shrew is my mentor."

Just then, the Sandman arrived in camp, back from his stroll, and was surprised to see all the new faces. Madam Mum made the introductions.

Then Madam Shrew introduced the trolls to them all. "This is Earl and Edna, and their daughter Esmerelda."

They didn't have time to exchange pleasantries or visit because the trolls were getting restless.

The father troll said impatiently to Madam Shrew, "Esmerelda has been having daymares. These fairies must be causing them. Fairies are always around when there are problems."

Madam Shrew answered, "That's because fairies fix problems, Earl. Remember? Fairies are problem solvers and fixers. These fairies are here to help fix the bad dreams problem. They are going to meet with the Dream Spider in the morning. The Web of Dreams has been destroyed, and the Dream Spider will have to rebuild it."

The trolls looked impressed, and Edna said, "No one has ever seen the Dream Spider. Be careful. I've heard he is ferocious."

Then Earl told the fairies, "Sorry we jarred you. Esmerelda isn't the only one having bad dreams. Our troll neighbors, Carl and Cate, and their daughter Clementina, have been having bad dreams too. We saw them two days ago. They live over there."

All three trolls pointed in different directions to show where their neighbors lived. Earl cleared his throat and added, "Well, we can't exactly remember where they live; but we run into them every few days, so we know they live close by."

Next, the fairies, the Sandman, the trolls, and Madam Robin all sat down for a visit. The trolls pulled marshmallows out of their pockets and offered them to the fairies for roasting. And the fairies shared their raspberries and lemon jellybeans with the trolls.

The trolls had trouble understanding that one marshmallow was enough for all of the fairies to share, since the marshmallows were so large and the fairies so small. Eventually, the fairies gave up trying to explain and accepted the marshmallows gratefully. When each of the fairies had their very own large marshmallow, the trolls were satisfied and beamed happily at one another.

Each of the trolls had three jellybeans and two raspberries. They thanked the fairies graciously. As the fairies roasted marshmallow bits on small twigs, they visited with the trolls. Dragonfly noticed that Madam Shrew made a point to remind the trolls several times that the fairies were going to fix the problem, and that they were not the cause of it.

The trolls left after about an hour. As they said goodbye, Earl told them, "We are stacking pinecones tonight, and looking for toadstool rings." He sounded thrilled.

The trolls grinned and waved goodbye. Then, taking their bell jars with them, they trooped off through the trees.

As the trolls left, Madam Monarch smiled and told the others, "They might find a toadstool ring here tomorrow. Toadstool rings usually appear where fairies have had a gathering."

When it was time for the fairies to go to sleep, Dragonfly extinguished the fire with a little dirt, and they all settled into their soft niches with the blankets and pillows. Madam Shrew and Milkweed had also brought blankets and pillows and stayed with them. And the Sandman made up a nice pile of dried leaves to sleep in.

Marigold did not sleep well, worrying about her recurring nightmare. And Firefly woke up with every slight rustle of the Sandman's leaves. She couldn't get over the feeling that something else was very wrong.

Chapter Seven

The Dream Spider

The fairies woke and stretched at first light. Milkweed was even more beautiful in daylight. Her wings were the exact, pale green color of a milkweed pod; and her sparkling, milkweed-strand dress shone brightly with the sunrise.

After a quick breakfast of powdered sugar puff pastries and the last of the raspberries, the fairies packed up camp and set off on the owl and falcon. They had obviously been very close to the spider's home because they were only in the air a few minutes before landing.

The Dream Spider's lair was on a rocky hillside. The owl and falcon set down in front of a narrow rock crevice, which was partially covered by a large, oily-black spider web.

As the fairies approached the crevice, they noticed that the web swayed slowly and rhythmically in the morning breezes. Dragonfly took the lead, with Madam Mum close behind her.

Hovering by the edge of the web, Dragonfly called to the spider. "Mr. Dream Spider! Please come out. We need your help."

Instantly, the Dream Spider appeared at the mouth of the rock crevice. This was the largest spider any of the group had ever seen. The Dream Spider had a huge, fat, furry black body with bands of many different colors on his long legs. He was about five inches high and eight inches wide.

Dragonfly flew a little closer to the Dream Spider and hovered in front of his head, saying, "Hello. We have been sent by Mother Nature to ask for your help."

Before she could go on, the Dream Spider spoke. His voice was so deep and dark, it sounded like smooth thunder. "I am on holiday, young lady, and I don't like being disturbed."

Dragonfly swallowed, then said, "I am sorry to disturb you, but the Web of Dreams has been destroyed. Nightmares are running rampant, and the doves are exhausted from working overtime. We need you to rebuild the web as soon as possible."

As she finished speaking, Dragonfly backed slowly away. But she was so intent on keeping her eyes on the Dream Spider that she didn't notice how close she was getting to the corner of his web. At the very edge, the web fluttered a little with the morning breeze and caught Dragonfly's foot. She tried to pull away and free her foot, but only succeeded in getting the other foot stuck as well. The Dream Spider moved slowly towards her.

The Sandman, owl, falcon, Madam Robin, and most of the fairies stared in horror. But Thistle lunged forward and placed herself protectively between Dragonfly and the spider. She pointed her quill wand at him and shouted, "Stay back, or I will poke and prickle you!" She then made several very quick sword-like jabs at the spider, and warned him, "I am very capable!"

Marigold was standing a little behind Madam Mum. She was terrified. Her nightmare was playing out in real life directly in front of her. She was even more frightened than she had been in her dream, and as feared, she was frozen in place, unable to move a muscle.

But there was another feeling inside her that she had not felt in her dream. It was like a surge of strength and power, growing and building up. After a few seconds, it seemed as though courage and confidence were spilling out of her ears. Without even thinking, she flew quickly forward and hovered shoulder to shoulder with Thistle in front of Dragonfly.

The Dream Spider had advanced to within a few inches of them. Thistle continued to slash forward with her wand in an effort to ward him off. Without even using her wand, Marigold slowly raised her right hand as though placing it flat on a wall. The force that came out of her hand caused the Dream Spider to slide backwards several inches. She kept her hand raised. Both Thistle and Marigold stood their ground, and the spider kept his distance. Madam Mum moved forward and tried to free Dragonfly from the web. But as hard as she pulled, her granddaughter stayed stuck.

After a few moments the spider spoke. "I wasn't going to hurt her. I was going to help her get loose." He paused as the fairies

eyed him suspiciously. Then he went on. "I don't eat fairies. Now, if you had brought some nice plump brownies with you, I might be tempted."

The fairies all stared at him in horror, imagining him eating their brownie friends.

"I'm joking," the spider said flatly. Then he added in an almost bored tone, "I don't eat brownies, or robins, or sand people. In fact, I'm a vegetarian."

"Impossible!" said Dragonfly. "I have never heard of a vegetarian spider."

The Dream Spider responded, "Have you ever heard of a spider that could talk?" The fairies did not reply, and the spider added, "Just a little pixie dust on her feet should do it."

Madam Mum reached into her belt pouch and sprinkled a bit of glittering pixie dust on Dragonfly's feet. She was immediately released.

The fairies all backed away from the web, and Dragonfly said, "Thank you."

"You're welcome," the spider replied. Then he addressed Marigold. "Be careful using your gift, little Marigold. It is very powerful. You gave me quite a hard push, and I am rather large. You wouldn't want to accidentally squash a grasshopper just because he looked at you funny."

Marigold nodded in agreement. Since she had never used her gift before, she had no idea the strength of her power. She hadn't meant to shove the Dream Spider so hard.

Before anyone could say anything else, the Sandman moved forward. With a long sweep of his arm, he tossed sand into the eyes of Madam Robin, Madam Shrew, Milkweed, Thistle, and Madam Monarch. Instantly, they all dropped to the ground in a deep sleep.

"What are you doing?" cried Dragonfly.

His hand deep in his bag of sand again, the Sandman answered, "I have private business with the Dream Spider." There was a dark gleam in his eyes.

Too late, Dragonfly realized that something was terribly wrong. She got hit with sand in her eyes at the same time as Madam Mum, Marigold, Firefly, the falcon, and the owl. They all went down.

Then the Sandman advanced towards the Dream Spider, who had kept very still, silently studying the scene. But the Sandman didn't have a chance to toss sand at the Dream Spider. Dragonfly and Madam Mum had only been stunned by the sand, and were not asleep. They jumped up and flew at the Sandman. With one of her best soccer moves, Dragonfly kicked the bag of sand out of his hands. It landed several feet away, well out of reach of the Sandman.

Madam Mum followed Dragonfly, and raising her pine needle wand, she shouted, "*FREEZE!*" A thin, glittering stream of

blue light shot out of her wand, immobilizing the Sandman.

"How can this be?" he cried. "I hit you with sand. Why aren't you asleep?"

Madam Mum laughed as she answered. "I've been on caffeine for about fifty years. You would have to hit me with something stronger than sleep sand to put me down."

And Dragonfly chimed in, "I never get to sleep easily or quickly. I've had insomnia since I was three. So your sand tricks won't work on me either."

The Sandman was quiet after this. Madam Mum hovered very close to his face and spoke coldly to him. "What is going on?" she asked. "We trusted you, Sandman."

When he still didn't answer, the Dream Spider approached. Looking closely at the Sandman, the spider spoke calmly. "This is not really the Sandman."

The dark gleam in the Sandman's eyes became even darker. Madam Mum looked keenly at him and finally understood. She backed up a little, closed her eyes, pointed her wand, and softly uttered the word, "*Evict.*"

Gray steam hissed from her wand and covered the Sandman in a dark, sooty cloud. After some coughing and choking, blackness began streaming out of the Sandman's eyes, ears, nose, and mouth.

When the streams of black had left him, the Sandman collapsed like a puppet that had lost its strings. Next, the oozing blackness came together, and took the shape of a creature very much like a small gremlin with large pointy ears, a lumpy body, and sharp teeth and claws.

The Dream Spider acted quickly. From his spinners, he shot long strings of inky-black web at the creature. The web strings whizzed by so quickly that Dragonfly and Madam Mum were knocked backwards several feet. In less than a minute, the black

creature was covered up to his neck with a cocoon of the spider's web.

"Drommelak..." the Dream Spider said in a matter-of-fact tone of voice, "the evil dream spirit who causes nightmares. I should have known." The spider inspected his cocoon closely. "I think this will hold, but it's a little loose around the neck. I don't want him wriggling out. I'll have to try to find something to reinforce this."

"Would this work?" Dragonfly asked, pulling the rubber canning ring out of her pocket.

"Perfect," said the Dream Spider, tying the ring tightly around the neck area of the cocoon with his long front legs.

Dragonfly was very pleased that the item she had been unable to recycle was put to good use.

The real Sandman was stirring and groaning. He sat up and looked around at the birds and fairies. "Is anyone hurt?" he asked.

"No. They are only asleep," the Dream Spider replied.

Then the Sandman put his face in his hands and wept. After a few moments, he collected himself and spoke. "Drommelak possessed me two weeks ago. He was in total command. I couldn't control my own actions." The Sandman paused for a moment, shaking his head before going on. "I destroyed the Web of Dreams. Drommelak came after me because I knew the location. Then he possessed me and made me go to the web. And he was going to try to kill you, so you couldn't rebuild it. I'm so sorry." The Sandman was shaking and upset, and again he put his face in his hands.

The Dream Spider said sympathetically, "It's not your fault." Then his voice became quiet and dangerous as he turned to Drommelak and added menacingly, "You are the reason for all of this. You destroyed my web, produced excess nightmares, made the doves work overtime, caused the Sandman pain and grief, and cut short my holiday. And the fairies have had to make a dangerous journey."

Even though he was angry, the spider's dark voice was very low and soft. "Well, you will have to explain yourself to Mother Nature. I will personally deliver you to her on my way to rebuild the Web of Dreams. I happen to know that she is in hurricane form right now, down in the Gulf. So that should be a lot of fun for you. Maybe you will learn a lesson."

The evil spirit's enormous black eyes widened with fear, and he whimpered a little.

Swinging the cocoon onto his back, the Dream Spider told Dragonfly and Madam Mum, "I will rebuild the web as quickly as I can."

"Do you need transportation?" Dragonfly asked. "I'm sure the barn owl would be happy to carry you."

The spider gave a low, dark laugh that was like a slow rumble of thunder. "No," he said. "But thank you. I travel much faster than birds, my dear. Farewell," he added.

With that, the Dream Spider was off. And he wasn't exaggerating about his speed. Dragonfly and Madam Mum only saw him for about two seconds before he streaked away like a large black arrow and was quickly lost from sight.

Next, Madam Mum instructed Dragonfly on how to wake the fairies and birds. "The sand affected their eyes and heads, so we can't start there. The sleep spell will be too strong. We must start with their toes. Sprinkle pixie dust on their feet, point your wand, and say, "*Awake.*"

After doing this to each of the birds and fairies, Dragonfly and Madam Mum watched and waited. Several minutes later, the fairies' and birds' toes began to wriggle. Then their legs moved. Eventually, the fairy spell worked its way all the way up to their faces, and everyone was waking, yawning, and stretching.

Dragonfly, Madam Mum, and the Sandman, who had recovered somewhat from his ordeal, told everyone what had happened.

Anxious to return home, the fairies said goodbye to Milkweed and Madam Shrew, thanking them for their help, especially with the trolls. Then the group set off on the owl and falcon.

Chapter Eight

Home to Better Dreams

On the return trip, the fairies talked to the Sandman. "I felt something was wrong," Firefly said, looking at him. "Too bad I couldn't tell *what* was wrong. We might have been able to do something sooner."

Madam Mum answered her. "No, dear. We might not have been able to handle Drommelak ourselves. We needed the Dream Spider's help. It's best that it happened this way."

Marigold told everyone, "My nightmares were not really dreams. I actually saw what was going to happen ahead of time: Dragonfly getting stuck in the web, and Thistle trying to help her. I don't understand."

They thought for a while, then Madam Monarch spoke. "I think we can credit your dreams of the future to the oak tree outside your bedroom window. Since oak trees can see the future, your dreams took the form of visions of actual events."

"That makes sense," Marigold said.

Early evening, the owl and falcon set down in the woods outside of town to drop off the Sandman. He told them, "I'm glad I got to meet all of you. Thank you so much for everything." Before saying goodbye, he added, "I wanted to tell you about a friend of mine – a starfish fairy. I visit with her when I collect dream sand in the Gulf. We make sand pictures together. You know, when you fall backwards in the sand and wave your arms about. Then you get up and see what kind of picture you made." The Sandman laughed a little and added,

"There aren't many other fairies down there, and she is very lonely. Maybe I could bring Starfish to one of your Fairy Circles."

Madam Mum answered, "I will talk to Madam Toad about inviting her. I don't know who is head of her region, but I'm sure a visit could be arranged. It is a very good idea to get to know fairies in other areas. We were lucky to meet Milkweed and Madam Shrew." All the fairies nodded in agreement.

Next, the birds took all of the fairies to Madam Monarch's home. The fairies thanked the owl and falcon many times for their help, and the birds departed.

Madam Mum and Madam Monarch ordered pizzas; and everyone had a wonderful dinner of salad, pizza, and root beer. They sat up for a while, discussing their adventure and eating lemon jellybeans. Then the fairies brushed their teeth and went to bed, tired but feeling good.

Across town, Mr. Wimple was returning home after the Garden Gnome Convention. He was very pleased and happy. His pockets and pant cuffs were full of seeds, roots, bulbs, and tools. He had a special new pair of breathable gardening gloves and a foldable trowel. He had also learned a new colorization technique for tulips that involved highly secret, concentrated gnome magic. The gnome inventors had done well this year.

On the Saturday following their adventure, Dragonfly received a nut message first thing in the morning from Milkweed. A small bluebird delivered the hazelnut to Jennifer's bedroom windowsill:

> *Jennifer,*
>
> *I was so happy to get to meet you. We are having a special fall Fairy Circle, the first Saturday in October. Please let me know if you and your grandmother can come. I*

will talk to the brownies and arrange

transportation for you.

Your friend,

Caitlin

Jennifer and her grandmother went out into the garden early to see Mr. Wimple. He was proudly showing them his new gloves and trowel when the Dream Spider suddenly appeared in the garden.

"Wow!" said Mr. Wimple. "I've never seen the likes of you around here before."

Jennifer introduced the Dream Spider to Mr. Wimple.

As Mr. Wimple went off to continue his work, the spider told Jennifer and her grandmother, "I just finished the new Web of Dreams. I thought you two might like to see it. It is in a new location not far from here. But if I take you there, you must promise never to tell anyone of its location. And you cannot return to see it again." They quickly agreed, nodding and smiling.

Jennifer ran inside the house to tell her mother that she and Grandmum would be taking a walk. Outside the front gate, and out of sight of the house, they changed into fairy form and followed the spider through fields and over hills.

In a remote area of overgrown woods, they came upon an old bell tower in a small clearing. There were several crumbling foundation blocks and stones strewn about the ground, but no building remained. Whether there had been an old school or church there, they couldn't tell. But the bell tower was still in good shape. It was made of large stones and had iron gridwork inside. Dragonfly and Madam Mum flew all the way to the top, following the Dream Spider. At the very peak of the tower, under the domed roof, was the Web of Dreams.

This was unlike any spider web Dragonfly had ever seen. It was very small, less than one inch in size, and was many times more intricate than a regular spider web. Dragonfly had assumed that the Web of Dreams would be black, like the spider's own web at home. But this web was spun of delicate, silky stands that were multicolored. Each strand had at least a hundred tiny sections of color. The Web of Dreams was every color they had ever seen, and more.

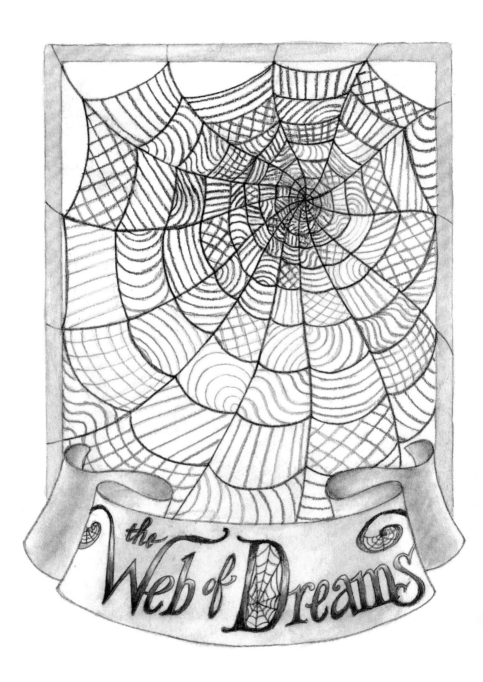

the Web of Dreams

At regular intervals, the individual colors in the web would flash. The fairies saw fuchsia, lime, violet, orange, lavender, and turquoise flashes. And the Dream Spider told them, "It's catching the bad dreams of day sleepers. You should see it at night. It's like a fireworks display."

As she watched, Dragonfly was overwhelmed by the beauty of the tiny Web of Dreams. With tears in her eyes, she turned away, gasping, "It's so beautiful."

The Dream Spider cleared his throat and said, "Well, I didn't mean to shake you up. I just thought you might like to see it."

Trying to get past the lump in her throat, Dragonfly choked out, "It's so small."

The spider answered, "Bigger isn't always better. In fact, size doesn't matter. For example, you are not very large, and look what you've accomplished." He cleared his throat again and added, "I don't know many little girls, or dragonflies, Jennifer.

the Dream Spider

I am pleased to call you my friend." Dragonfly smiled and shook hands with one of the Dream Spider's front legs. It was soft and furry, not at all itchy and scratchy like she had imagined it would be.

As the Dream Spider left, he said one final thing. "By the way, I really am a vegetarian. Broccoli and artichokes are my favorite foods." Dragonfly and Madam Mum both laughed and waved as the spider streaked away.

At home that evening, Jennifer sent a nut message to the Dream Spider, thanking him for showing them the web.

Two days later, she received the walnut back. Inside was a tiny, braided bracelet made from silky multicolored strands of web, just like those in the Web of Dreams. Jennifer cradled and stroked the precious gift. She found it easier to fall asleep that night, and had a very pleasant dream.

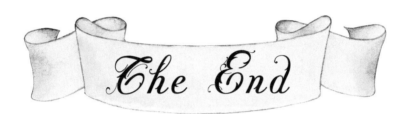

The End

Fairy Fun

Boots
By J.H. Sweet

Dad used to put his old boots in the garden
to scare the rabbits away.
For years, I wondered if it really worked.
Cool and dewy April morning,
sitting on the porch,
misty gray clouds holding off the sun.
A small gray cottontail skips by,
sniffs a boot, and turns to me to say,
"Thanks anyway, not my size."

Make A Dream Bracelet:

If you would like to create a Dream Bracelet for yourself just like the one the Dream Spider gave to Dragonfly, you can follow these ten easy steps. Make sure you have your parent's permission to do this before you begin.

To begin, you will need:
6 strands of embroidery floss, each 25" long.
   (Use as many or as few colors as you like, but remember the Web of Dreams has many different colors...)
Scissors
Masking tape

continued on the next page

DREAMS

1). Use your scissors to cut six 25" long strands of embroidery floss. Each strand is part of the word **"DREAMS."**

2). Hold the ends of the all six strands and tie a knot leaving a 3-4" tail on the end.

3). Now, tape the knotted end to a table, back of a chair or anywhere your parents recommend.

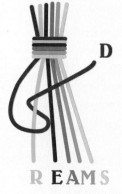

R EAMS

D

4). The strand on the far left is strand **D**. Pick it up and loop it over and then under the strand to its right, strand **R,** to make a knot. It is just like the first knot when tying your shoes. Hold strand **R** straight and pull up on strand **D** to pull the knot snug to the top.

5). Make a second knot exactly the same way using the same strands (**D** and R).

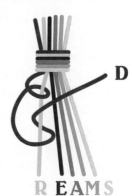

6). Now you can let go of strand R. Now loop strand **D** over and under strand **E** to make a knot. Do it again. Make sure that you are pulling each new knot snugly to the top.

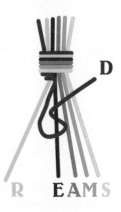

7). Repeat this process for strands **A**, **M** and, finally, S. If you did this correctly, strand **D**, will now be on the far right. Congratulations, you have completed your first row!

DREAMS

8). The first string on the left is now strand **R**. Pick that up and repeat steps 4 through 7. After each row, the strand you started with on the far left will be the strand that ends up on the far right.

9). Make sure that the bracelet long enough to fit around your wrist and when you are done, you can trim the tail on top down if you want to.

10). Sleep well, enjoy your dreams and remember that you are now protected by the Dream Spider and the powerful Web of Dreams!

FAIRY FACTS

Peafowl

Male peafowl are called peacocks and are known for their showy feathers. The females are called peahens and have smaller, less colorful feathers. Peafowl feathers are often called plumage, and the peacock's long tail is sometimes called a train. These large birds are related to pheasants and turkeys and are found in many countries around the world. Wild peafowl like to eat snakes and small rodents.

Morgan-le-Fay

In many ways this is one of the most famous fairies of all time. She is King Arthur's most important enemy and his half-sister. Her name means Morgan the Fay, or in modern English, Morgan the Fairy. While she is Arthur's enemy, in one of the most common stories about Arthur, the day he is badly wounded she takes him aboard a ship and sets sail for the magical island of Avalon. There, it is said, Morgan the Fairy and four other fairy queens guard Arthur until the time when the world is in such peril that he will set sail again from Avalon to help save the world.

Inside you is the power to do anything

The Fairy Chronicles

. . . the adventures continue

Marigold and the Feather of Hope

Like most nine year old girls, Beth wants to spend her summer goofing off. Unfortunately her parents are making her spend two whole weeks with her crazy Aunt Evelyn. This time however, Aunt Evelyn has a secret to tell...

Somewhat alarmed, Beth slid sideways in her seat putting about a foot of extra distance between her and her aunt. Aunt Evelyn was leaning forward, obviously very excited about something. Her dark brown eyes, now flashing with flecks of orange and black, were a bit scary. Beth had never seen these colors in her aunt's eyes before. They both took a deep breath, staring at each other as the room became very still.

Beth felt a tingling sensation, as though something very important was about to happen. Aunt Evelyn continued to stare at her. Just as Beth was thinking of having another sip of soda, her aunt stated calmly, "You are a marigold fairy."

Discovering her new powers, making new and magical friends and being sent on a super important mission make for one really exciting summer. But if Beth, now known as Marigold, doesn't find the Feather of Hope it might be the last good summer anyone ever has.

Now Available in Bookstores and Online

Thistle and the Shell of Laughter

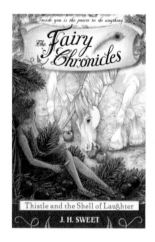

Thistle and the Shell of Laughter

J. H. SWEET

The Shell of Laughter has been stolen from Staid, the Elf! Madam Toad sends Thistle and her friends to recapture the Shell before all laughter is gone forever. But a very dangerous enemy has control of the Shell.

Killjoy Crosspatch, the Spirit of Sorrow, stared at them without speaking. Thistle, Marigold, and Dragonfly thought he was the most disgusting and foul creature they had ever seen. "Where is the shell?" demanded Staid.

Killjoy Crosspatch didn't speak. Instead, a wide, uneven smile crept across his ugly face, and he slowly raised his hands in front of him. From his dripping palms, a dark gray, smoky cloud began to seep. It slowly crept towards the elf, the hedgehog, the leprechaun, Madam Robin, and the fairies.

They tried to take cover behind several of the rocks, but the oozing darkness followed them. It seemed there was no escape from the cloud of sorrow.

Can they do it? Will the fairies defeat the Spirit of Sorrow and return the Shell to its rightful owner? More important, will the world ever get to laugh again?

Coming in July 2007

Firefly and the Quest of the Black Squirrel

Firefly and the Quest of the Black Squirrel

J. H. SWEET

Firefly and her friends are going on a camping trip. But little do they know that they are about to be sent on a real adventure, where the stakes are nothing less than the future of all the species on Earth.

The black squirrel looked nervous. When he spoke, his soft voice quavered a little at first. "I have made a long journey to be here because a terrible sickness has struck several black squirrel colonies in the far North, and it is spreading. The sickness causes death."

The black squirrel stopped his story for a moment. When he started speaking again, his voice shook. "But I haven't told you the worst part. The curse is a *Calendar-Chain-Curse,* set up to attack a new species each month. Next month, all white-tailed deer will die. In May, beavers, and the following month, earthworms. In July, snow geese, and so on. Eventually, it will reach humans. There is no stopping it." He sighed, "It is a *perfect curse.*"

This is a very dangerous mission and Madam Toad is dispatching some of her best fairies for this mission: Firefly, Thistle, Marigold, and their new friend Periwinkle. The girls will have to use all of their magic, brains, and brawn to stop the perfect curse!

Coming in July 2007

About the Author

J.H. Sweet has always looked for the magic in the everyday. She has an imaginary dog named Jellybean Ebenezer Beast. Her hobbies include hiking, photography, knitting, and basketry. She also enjoys watching a variety of movies and sports. Her favorite superhero is her husband, with Silver Surfer coming in a close second. She loves many of the same things the fairies love, including live oak trees, mockingbirds, weathered terra-cotta, butterflies, bees, and cypress knees. In the fairy game of "If I were a jellybean, what flavor would I be?" she would be green apple. J.H. Sweet lives with her husband in South Texas and has a degree in English from Texas State University.

About the Illustrator

Ever since she was a little girl, Tara Larsen Chang has been captivated by intricate illustrations in fairy tales and children's books. Since earning her BFA in Illustration from Brigham Young University, her illustrations have appeared in numerous children's books and magazines. When she is not drawing and painting in her studio, she can be found working in her gardens to make sure that there are plenty of havens for visiting fairies.